Mermaid KINGDOM

Raintree is an imprint of Capstone Global Library
Limited, a company incorporated in England and Wales
having its registered office at 7 Pilgrim Street, London,
EC4V 6LB – Registered company number: 6695582

www.raintree.co.uk
myorders@raintree.co.uk

Designed by Alison Thiele

Artistic Elements: Shutterstock

ISBN 978 1 4062 9296 1 (paperback)
18 17 16 15 14
10 9 8 7 6 5 4 3 2 1

British Library Cataloguing in Publication Data
A full catalogue record for this book is available from
the British Library.

Printed and bound in China.

Shyanna's
Wish

by Janet Gurtler

illustrated by Katie Wood

raintree
a Capstone company — publishers for children

Mermaid life

☆ Mermaid Kingdom refers to all the kingdoms in the sea, including Neptunia, Caspian, Hercules, Titania and Nessland. Each kingdom has a King and Queen who live in a castle. Merpeople live in caves.

☆ Mermaids get their legs on their thirteenth birthdays at the stroke of midnight. It's a celebration when the mermaid makes her first voyage onto land. After their thirteenth birthdays, mermaids can go onto land for short periods of time but must be very careful.

☆ If a mermaid goes onto land before her thirteenth birthday, she will get her legs early and never get her tail back. She will lose all memories of being a mermaid and will be human forever.

⭐ Mermaids are able to stay on land with legs for no more than forty-eight hours. Any longer and they will not be able to get their tails back and will be human forever. They will lose all memories of being a mermaid.

⭐ If they fall in love, merpeople and humans can marry and have babies (with special permission from the King and Queen of their kingdom). Their babies are half-human and half-merperson. However, this love must be the strongest love possible in order for it to be approved by the King and Queen.

⭐ Half-human mermaids are able to go on land indefinitely and can change back into a mermaid at any point. However, they are not allowed to tell other humans about the mermaid world unless they have special permission from the King and Queen.

Chapter one

It was almost the big day! Only one more night until my birthday! Everyone loves their birthday, but this year was extra special for me because I was going to be thirteen. In Mermaid Kingdom, your thirteenth birthday is a VBD (very big deal). At midnight on thirteenth birthdays, merpeople can go onto land and get to use legs for the first time. After that, our legs can be used on land for a few hours at a time. I was really looking forward to being able to join my best friends, Rachel and Cora, for adventures on land.

I loved being a mermaid and I loved the sea, but there was something about breathing air and having legs that intrigued me, too.

"Shyanna!" my mum called while I plaited my hair and imagined myself skipping on the beach.

"What's up, Mum?" I shouted from my room as I finished off my hair. I imagined she was curious about which song I'd selected to sing at my midnight leg ceremony. The leg ceremony was completely magical.

"Have you finished with the shell decorations you and the girls were making for the Neptunia Day parade?" my mum asked.

I rolled my eyes at the reflection in my mirror. The mirror was a treasure my dad had found in an old shipwreck. He'd given it to me just before he disappeared two years earlier.

Neptunia may have been the best kingdom in the sea, but there were always dangers underwater. From humans and nets to sharks and storms, the sea was a dangerous place to live. Anything could happen at any time, and nobody really knows what happened to my dad. Although it's getting easier, my mum and I still miss him every day.

"They're finished," I called. "We left them on the kitchen table."

"Thank goodness. We have to finish off all the details on the Queen's float this morning. You girls are lifesavers!" she called. "I was up so late last night going over all the last minute details with the parade committee. I never could have done them on my own." She swam into my room and smiled at me. "You look so beautiful." She swam closer and kissed me on the cheek. "I can't believe it's your last day as a twelve-year-old mergirl!"

Mum was always so busy on Neptunia Day because she was the leader of the parade committee. Unfortunately, this year Neptunia Day fell on the same day as my birthday. It was overshadowing my big day a bit, but I was trying hard not to let it ruin things.

We looked at each other in my mirror, and then she sighed. "I wish I wasn't so busy with the parade committee today. But I do have to finish off all the float preparations. The Queen likes things to be perfect. Speaking of perfect, we'll make all the final arrangements for your leg ceremony tonight. You must be so excited!"

"I really am, " I said. "I can't wait to have legs so I can go with Rachel and Cora to see Owen on land and meet his friends!"

Owen was Rachel's best friend and a human. Because Rachel was half-human and half-mermaid, she could go onto land whenever she wanted for as long as she wanted. That's how she met Owen. Rachel often felt a bit strange because she was both human and mermaid, but I thought it was amazing and I was a little bit jealous of her.

"Well, you won't see Owen and any of his friends at your leg ceremony," she said. "It's too late at night, and Owen and his friends will be asleep."

"I know that," I said. "I mean later. When I go onto land with Cora and Rachel. Also, I've decided to have a small leg ceremony. Just Rachel and Cora and their families."

"Sounds good," she said, but I could tell she wasn't concentrating.

"I'm so excited that you'll be coming onto the beach with me. I know it's been a long time for you," I continued, hoping to spend a little more time with my mum before she had to leave again.

"Mm hmm. Good." She nodded as she checked through the shell handbag slung over her shoulder. "So what are you doing today?"

"I'm meeting Cora and Rachel at Walrus Waterpark to go over my plans. We might go for a swim with the dolphins later or take Cora's sisters to watch the sea turtles."

"Oh no," my mum said, clearly not listening to me. "I forgot the list with the order of the parade floats." She swam closer and kissed my forehead again.

"I have to find it before I go. Sorry I'm so wrapped up in Neptunia Day," she added.

"It's okay," I said, even though I wished my birthday didn't coincide with Neptunia Day. It was a great day of celebration for our castle, with a big parade and lots of other fun events. It went on all day and late into the night. And I didn't want to seem selfish, but it seemed like with the preparations and timing, everyone was forgetting about my birthday. Thirteen was a really big event, and getting my legs for the first time would be incredible.

"I have to run," Mum said. "I'm so sorry, but we'll talk about everything you've planned at our spa appointment tomorrow. I'm so glad Rachel and Cora are around to help you with your plans. You're so lucky to have them. They're such great best friends." She wiped away a smear of algae on my mirror and frowned. "It's been such a long time since I've been on land." Her lips turned down more, and she sighed.

"I'll see you later. Have a good day," she said absently as she swam off to fetch the decorations.

My mum seemed even more distracted than usual, which didn't make me feel confident that my birthday plans would work out how I'd like them to. The leg ceremony was such a big thing, and without my mum I couldn't do it. Her distraction made me feel nervous – very, very nervous.

Chapter two

"Hello, almost-birthday girl!" Cora said as I swam into Walrus Waterpark. As always, Cora's baby sister was tucked under her arm and another sister swam in front of her, giggling as she tried to get away.

"I can't believe my mum volunteered to work with yours on the parade committee this year," Cora said. "Now I've got to look after my sisters all day long." She sighed dramatically as she put Jewel into the baby swing and then pushed her other two sisters.

For once I agreed with her. I loved Cora's sisters

despite all their shenanigans, but they were a lot of hard work. I always wished I had sisters of my own, but today I just wanted things to be about my birthday plans.

"Can you take them with us to swim with the dolphins later?" I asked, knowing the answer already. I swam over and took over Jewel's swing.

"No. They're too young. We'll have to do it another time," Cora said.

I nodded, trying not to show my disappointment. "I wonder where Rachel is," I said, looking around the park. "She's not usually late."

"She's been working on a new routine for the Spirit Squad," Cora said. "She's probably lost track of time."

Rachel was a bit obsessed with coming up with new routines for the group to perform. We were all on the squad, but Rachel was the most involved.

"Oh," I said, trying not to show the resentment that was creeping around my insides. I was upset that no one seemed to be very concerned about my birthday or seemed to want to help with my plans. I'd been looking forward to it for as long as I could remember. Your thirteenth birthday and your leg ceremony were so important, and nobody seemed to care. Not my mum, and not my best friends.

"What are you wearing to the parade?" Cora asked as she pushed one sister in the swing and swam over quickly to push the others next to her.

I sighed, sick of Neptunia Day and all its birthday attention robbing. I wanted to talk about what I should wear for my leg ceremony, not the silly parade. I wanted to talk about how I should do my hair and what colour I should paint my nails. I was so tired of talking about the parade, and it hadn't even started yet.

"I don't know," I said, rolling my eyes a little bit. "My mum and I are going to the spa before the parade, and I haven't really thought about it that much. I'm more concerned about what I'm going to wear that evening."

I was just about to tell Cora what happened with my mum and how I was feeling about my leg ceremony when Rachel swam into the park.

"Sorry I'm late!" she cried before I could mutter any more complaints about my birthday plans. Rachel swam to the swings and did a flip in front of the sisters to make them laugh. Her long red hair flowed out behind her. I wished I could get my hair to curl and spring freely like hers. It would be the perfect style for my leg ceremony.

"I was at Cassie's cave," Rachel said. Cassie was the songwriter for the Spirit Squad, and she and Rachel spent lots of time working together.

I was glad Rachel was making new friends. She'd had a horrible time with some of the merkids when she and her dad first moved to Neptunia. Most of us thought it was amazing that she was half-human and could use her legs on land whenever she wanted to. But some merkids hadn't been so nice, and Rachel sometimes found it difficult to trust.

I was glad Rachel loved the Spirit Squad and had made new friends, but was it wrong that I wanted some of her attention on me now?

Rachel and Cora both played with me for a while, but they were both really distracted. Before long they both left, and my birthday had hardly even been mentioned.

Chapter three

That night Mum got home late again. She was exhausted from all her hard work with the parade committee. We ate leftovers and decided to talk about my birthday plans in the morning because she was too tired. So much for getting everything ready for my birthday. I felt like nobody had time for me, and it was really starting to upset me.

Mum wanted to go to bed early, so I pretended I was tired too and ended up sadly staring at the ceiling until late into the night.

***

When I opened my eyes in the morning, I stretched my arms out and smiled. It was my birthday! I was thirteen! I would finally get my legs!

I swam out of bed. "Mum?" I called.

No one answered. The cave was quiet.

I swam out of my room. I swam into the kitchen. There was a note on the table next to a bowl and my favourite kind of cereal.

"Happy Birthday, Shyanna! I've had to nip out and look at a problem with the Queen's float. I'll be back as soon as I can. Make sure you're ready to go to the spa when I get home!"

Things were too silent and too dull. This was not how I wanted my birthday to start. I tried not to be disappointed and softly hummed the "Happy Birthday" song to myself as I ate. I tried to enjoy the peace and quiet.

After breakfast, I swam to the front garden.

It was even quiet out there. The only things I saw were some small snails playing a slow and noiseless game of hide-and-seek. I guessed that everyone was too busy getting things ready for Neptunia Day to care about my birthday.

I felt eyes on me and looked around hopefully, but it was only a scallop watching me. He was bright and beautiful with his fan-shaped shell, so I waved hello. I hoped he'd come over and offer some company, but he ignored my gesture and swam away, opening and closing his shell to move. I have never felt so lonely in my life!

I sighed, but then I heard the phone ringing from inside our cave. It had to be Rachel or Cora, and they'd probably burst into "Happy Birthday" as soon as I picked it up. I hurried inside and grabbed the phone with a big smile on my face.

"Hello?" I sang.

"Shyanna?" It was my mum. And I could tell she wasn't happy just by the way she said my name.

"Hi, Mum," I said. "Are you okay?

"I'm fine, Shy. Things have just gone a bit crazy here. We have a bit of an emergency. A hammerhead shark smashed up the Queen's float. We're working really hard to mend it, but I don't know how long I'm going to be delayed. I'm trying to get away, but there's no one else to manage things. Do you think … would you mind terribly if one of the girls went to the spa in my place? I feel so terrible, but I have no idea how long this will take, and I don't want you to miss your appointment because of me."

My heart sank to the bottom of the sea. "Of course not, Mum. Don't worry about it. I'll ask Rachel or Cora to come. It'll be fine. Fun!"

I didn't mention that we were supposed to finalize my plans for the leg ceremony. I still had to choose my song, and we hadn't worked out what Mum was going to wear to coordinate with my outfit for our first walk onto land together.

"Cora's mum is with me," Mum went on, "so

Cora's probably going to be busy looking after her sisters. I'm sure Rachel will love it, though! Have fun. I'll be home as soon as I can!" Then she hung up the phone.

A tear slid out of my eye as I put the phone down. She hadn't even said goodbye.

I called Rachel, but her dad answered. "Sorry, Shyanna," he said. "Rachel's gone to see Owen. He has some new songs to teach her, and she wanted to incorporate them into the new Spirit Squad routine. She really loves that group. But hey, happy birthday! Today's the big day! Can't wait to see you on your new legs tonight!"

"Thanks, Mr Marlin," I said, thankful that at least someone could find the time to wish me a happy birthday. I seriously considered asking him to go to the spa with me, but decided that would be far too awkward for both of us.

I sighed when I hung up the phone, feeling like the biggest loser in Mermaid Kingdom. It was my birthday, and I was all by myself! My birthday was a complete disaster.

I knew I could ask another mergirl to go with me to the spa. I had plenty of friends from school, and anyone would be happy to have a free spa date. But it didn't feel right to ask just anyone. Anyway, no one else had been invited to my leg ceremony. It seemed selfish and too last minute to ask someone else to join me to celebrate now.

I'd have to go alone. How awful could it be?

Chapter four

"You'll start your song quietly as you emerge from the water at exactly midnight," Star Fishery, the beautician at the spa explained as she painted my fingernails.

Star had been thrilled when she found out it was my birthday. She actually shrieked loudly with joy when I told her I was thirteen. When she heard about my mum's emergency, she immediately started helping me plan my leg ceremony. She even helped me decide on my song and insisted that I rehearse it.

Despite my stage fright and all the other mermaids in the spa, I managed to sing the whole thing out loud. Everyone clapped when I had finished and assured me I would have the most perfect leg ceremony ever.

"When you get your legs, you start to build up the song at a louder crescendo. The moon is full tonight, so you'll be lit by soft glowing light," Star said. "We'll undo your plaits so your hair will flow all curly and bouncy around your pretty face." She giggled with delight, and her enthusiasm was infectious and warmed my woeful heart. "It will be magical – completely magical and unforgettable. The way every leg ceremony is meant to be."

"Do you really think so?" I asked, starting to feel a lot better about my special day. Leave it to Star to bring the magic back.

"I do," she said. "I know you wish your mum was here, but I'm going to help you and make you so beautiful it will be a night you'll never forget.

What colour is your outfit? I'll apply matching starfish decorations to your nails!"

I told her what I planned to wear: the purple shell top and matching necklaces. She nodded with enthusiasm. She rubbed my tail with sparkly oil and added rainbow glitter to my hair. She said the hair glitter would last all day and shimmer in the light of the full moon. The excitement in the spa helped me get in the mood for the day, and my sadness about being forgotten disappeared.

As I got up from the chair, everyone cheered and whistled. Then Star started off a round of "Happy Birthday" and everyone sang. I floated out of the shop and swam back towards my cave, finally feeling special and happy.

With all the extra work Star had put in at the spa, I was home a bit later than expected. I swam in the front door of the cave, excited to show my mum how incredible I looked.

"Mum!" I sang when I swam into our cave,

already holding out my hand so she could admire my birthday nails. I wasn't going to dwell on the fact that it was the mermaid at the spa who had helped me plan the final details of my leg ceremony. Nothing could take away from my big day now! Everything was organized and it was going to be perfect.

"Mum?" I shouted again.

There was no answer. In fact, our cave was eerily quiet.

I swam into the kitchen. "Mum?" I said, but no one said a word. I swam around the cave and realized, with heart-crushing certainty, that she hadn't come home yet.

There was no clam cake. There were no sea balloons or presents on the table. The Neptunia Day parade was more important to her than I was. All of my excitement from the spa evaporated in one big sigh.

I didn't want to cry, but I could barely hold back the tears anymore.

I grabbed the phone and called Rachel's cave.
Perhaps her dad knew where my mum was. No one at
the Marlin cave answered. I frowned and then dialed
Cora's number. No one answered there, either. Were
they all out enjoying the Neptunia Day festivities
without me? Had they completely forgotten about my
birthday? I glanced at the clock as I put the phone
back onto the table.

It was already past tea time, and I hadn't heard
from my two best friends or my mum for hours. I
swam slowly to my room, catching a reflection of my
shimmering tail in my special mirror on the
cave wall.

If my dad was here, would I be all alone on my
thirteenth birthday? I swam into my bedroom, my
heart heavy and tears bubbling up in the corners of
my eyes.

"Shyanna!" a voice shouted from outside the cave.

I frowned. Was that Rachel's voice? It sounded
panicked.

I swam towards my door as Rachel burst inside.

"Rachel!" I cried. Finally, someone had come to see me on my birthday! But then I saw her face. It was pale and worried. She didn't look happy or excited. She looked terrified. What was going on?

"Thank goodness you're here!" she said.

I frowned, but before I could ask what was wrong, she grabbed my hand and pulled me.

"Come on. We have to go. Now! Jewel is trapped in a fishing net!" she shouted. "We're too big to get her out. We need you. You're her last hope."

Chapter five

My heart pounded like waves crashing onto the beach as Rachel and I swam up through the water to the fishing net where Jewel was stuck.

"Cora and I have tried to get her out, but we're too big," Rachel explained as we swam faster than I thought possible. "You are the only one small enough to help her. Your mum is there, and my dad and Cora's family, but no one can get to her."

"What was everyone doing when she got stuck?" I asked.

She glanced at me. "I'll explain later."

We swam so quickly that everything was a blur, and in a few minutes we reached the net. My tail ached, and the shine and shimmer from the spa had completely disappeared from kicking so hard, but none of that mattered when I saw Jewel.

Baby Jewel was inside a net, trapped and squished up against hundreds of fish of various sizes. Her whole family and my mum and Rachel's dad were gathered outside of the net, following it with terrified helpless looks on their faces as it dragged along the sea floor. It was eerily quiet as the net moved, like an awful nightmare. All the nearby sea creatures were hiding, frightened.

Cora swam to my side the instant she saw me. "Oh, Shyanna!" she cried. "We've tried and tried, but we're too big to get into the net. Jewel can't get out by herself. She doesn't understand how, and she's too stressed out to follow instructions. She needs someone to go in and get her."

"I'll go," I said without hesitation. Being small for my age was finally a benefit. As well as being small, I was really flexible. It was my time to step up and help.

"Be careful, Shyanna," my mum said, patting my shoulder as I swam by.

Cora's mum had three little mergirls clinging to her, and Cora's dad had his arm around her. "Please help," he whispered. I nodded and swam past. There was no time to talk. Rachel and Cora swam with me to the net.

"If you can slip inside the hole, you can help get Jewel out," Cora said. Her voice was strained and nervous. "You have to get her out!"

I nodded and swam to the net, grabbing at the thick scratchy rope. It pulled away from my hands as if it sensed what I was about to do, almost pulling my fingernails off.

"Oh!" I shouted, surprised. When I pulled my hand back, I caught a glimpse of my nails. My new manicure was destroyed, but I knew that didn't matter. The only thing that mattered at that moment was Jewel.

"The boat is trolling, so it will sometimes make sudden moves like that," Cora told me. "It's okay. Try again. Hurry."

I nodded and swam to the rope. It was rough and wiry and totally inflexible. No wonder the girls couldn't break through. I glanced around at the holes to see if some were bigger than others. There was one that seemed a bit larger. It was going to be a tight fit, but I knew I could do it.

I squeezed my head in without too much of a problem and then wiggled around and got my body through. The rope scratched and burned my tail, but I ignored the pain and reached down. My fins were cut up and sore, but I remembered a trick from when I used to play hide-and-seek. I took a deep breath and folded my tail in half.

I was in!

"Jewel!" I cried and started shoving fish out of my way.

Jewel was crying. Her tail was tangled in the rope, and she couldn't swim away from it. Fish were pressed against each other, all of them struggling to get out and causing an even bigger tangle.

I gritted my teeth and pushed myself through the fish to get to Jewel. I wrapped my arms around her and tugged, but she shrieked loudly when I pulled her. I had to get closer to free her tail.

Outside the net I heard the girls shouting, and our mothers' cries got louder and louder. I didn't pay any attention. I had to focus on Jewel. As gently as I could, I untied Jewel from the net and then held her in my arms.

"Hello, little one," I said and smiled to try and calm her down.

"Shyanna!" Cora called.

I looked through layers of fish at the holes in the thick rope as I held Jewel close. "You're moving,"

40

Cora cried, pointing up. "The net is being pulled to the surface. You need to hurry!"

I realized Cora was swimming higher as she yelled, her tail wiggling fast to keep up with the net as it was being pulled closer to the surface. Rachel was a few feet below her, swimming strongly to try to catch up.

"Get out!" Cora shouted. "You have to get out before you reach the surface or the humans will see you!"

I squeezed through thousands of little fish and dove towards the bottom of the net, holding Jewel tightly in my arms.

"The net is almost out of the water!" Cora cried. "No!"

Chapter six

I put my head down and swam faster, protecting Jewel with my arms. I managed to squeeze through a wall of fish, and my head popped through a hole. I was going to make it! I pushed my way through and was about to fold my fin to finish my escape from the net when Jewel screamed. Her torn tail was caught on the wiry rope again.

I gently tugged her, trying to pull her through, but she cried louder. I glanced up in a panic. The rope was almost out of the water. I could see the reflection of the sun from below the water. We were close to the surface, and I was starting to panic.

I struggled to free Jewel without hurting her as we continued to move up. I held my breath. There was no way I was going to let her go on her own. Merpeople were yelling beneath us, but I didn't stop trying. I finally managed to pull her tail free, but a split second later realized that it was too late. The top of my head was already out of the water.

Around me, the fish gasped. They couldn't breathe out of the water, because they were unable to adapt to oxygen from air the way merpeople could. I closed my eyes and waited to be exposed. We were going to be pulled out of the water, and there was nothing I could do about it. It wouldn't be long before the fishermen realized they'd caught more than a net full of fish.

Humans still thought merpeople were just legends. Once the humans spotted us, we would risk exposing the underwater world and put all merpeople

in danger. The Kings and Queens of Mermaid Kingdom couldn't allow that to happen, which was why they had created a magic spell. If we were exposed to humans and were caught, we would lose our tails and memories of being mermaids. We would be human forever, never able to return to the sea. It would appear as though the fishermen had caught a young human girl and a baby. If we were spotted but managed to escape, we would never be able to get legs. We would never be able to leave the sea.

Everything was happening so quickly. I closed my eyes as I waited to be pulled up to the surface. It was my thirteenth birthday. The day that was supposed to be the happiest day of my life. Instead, I was trapped in a net, about to be exposed to humans and lose all my memories – and all of my family and friends.

With renewed energy and panic, I opened my eyes, dipped my head underwater, pulled on Jewel, and managed to force our way to the bottom of the net and out of a small hole.

Suddenly there were loud noises from the boat above us. Something was causing a huge commotion. There was shouting and waves, and then a beautiful sound that was a little muffled under the water. As quickly as it had begun, the commotion stopped.

The net dropped and sank quickly. The top of the net opened as we sailed downwards. I held tightly onto Jewel and swam out, following a big, excited school of fish to safety. It was a miracle!

"We're free!" I shouted when we were free of the net. "We're safe, Jewel!"

I did a couple of victory flips, and Jewel stopped crying. She started to giggle. Then I swam over to Cora, who was watching us with wide eyes. I held out Jewel. Cora took her baby sister from me and hugged her tightly.

When she looked up at me, there were tears spilling down her cheeks. She blinked quickly as she stared at me and then looked up towards the surface of the water.

"I'm so sorry, Shy," she said.

"What's wrong?" I frowned and glanced at Rachel to see what was going on, but she was crying, too.

"Your mum..." Cora said.

That was the sound I'd heard.

A sound I hadn't heard in a very, very long time, since before my dad disappeared.

It was my mum, singing.

Chapter seven

"What's happened?" I demanded, feeling even more panicked than I had felt when I was trapped in the net with Jewel.

Cora was holding Jewel tightly. "Your mum was very brave. She saved you. She saved you and Jewel." Cora's family and Rachel's dad were swimming closer to us, shouting my name and Jewel's. But all I could think about was my mum.

I glanced down at the sea below from where they approached. Large strands of coral reef stretched up

as if waving, and bright blue-cheeked butterflyfish swarmed around them. The scene was colourful and deceptively beautiful. Up swam Cora's parents, their eyes on Jewel, looking relieved and exhausted. But when they glanced at me, I saw the tears and sadness in their eyes. Cora's mum grabbed Jewel from Cora's arms, crying and holding her tightly.

"Oh, Shyanna, thank you," she whispered.

"Where's my mum?" I shouted at everyone and no one at the same time, with a very bad feeling in my fins. I knew. I knew where she was, but nobody would say it.

"She said she was going to cause a distraction," Rachel's dad said quietly.

Cora's dad swam up close to me and patted my arm. "Oh, Shyanna, you saved Jewel. You saved our baby."

"Where's my mum?" I shouted again, my dread growing as I looked around at all the beautiful sea life surrounding me.

"She said she was going to shock the fishermen so they'd drop the net," Rachel's dad said. "We couldn't stop her. She swam out of the water, and she started to sing."

"It was her," I whispered.

"It was the most powerful thing I've ever heard," Rachel's dad said, his eyes sad but also filled with wonder. "I've never heard anything so beautiful in my life, and we were below the water. The humans above the water were so mesmerized by her singing that they dropped the net."

"But she didn't need to do that," I said. "I had managed to get free and save Jewel."

"What a voice," Rachel's dad repeated, and everyone nodded solemnly.

I swallowed. "So my mum was seen by the humans? Singing?"

"She was," Rachel's dad said.

"And she's still up there?" I asked, barely able to get the words out.

"No." We all turned to see Rachel. She was breathing heavily. "I swam up. She wasn't in the boat. They saw her, but she stayed on a rock and escaped before they broke out of her spell."

"Thank goodness!" I sighed with relief. I had been thinking the absolute worst. I knew she would never be able to use her legs again, but at least she was alive!

"She's trapped in the sea now, forever," Rachel said sadly.

"Where is she?" I asked.

"The King and Queen are with her. They left the Neptunia Day celebrations and came straight away," Rachel said.

"Are they already here?" I asked. It seemed like it had all happened so quickly. It *had* all happened so quickly.

Rachel nodded. "The magic used is serious. They were here within seconds. They had to make sure Neptunia was safe."

"But she saved me. She saved Jewel," I whispered.

"I know," Rachel said. "But it's an offence, Shy. Exposing herself to humans. She got away, but the King and Queen don't know if the humans realized what she was. They don't think anyone will believe the fishermen if they talk about what they saw. But rules are rules. She was seen. She'll never be able to use her legs on land again."

Chapter eight

I swam up closer to the surface. The sunset was rippling over the water above, creating a gorgeous array of colours. There was no wind and no waves. It was completely still and quiet. The boat was gone. There was no sign of the King and Queen or my mum. It was eerie.

"They must have gone back to the palace," Rachel said.

"I have to get to her," I cried. "I have to see my mum!"

My shredded tail hurt from scraping the rope and folding up to escape, but I moved through the water faster than a shark on a hunt. I had never swam so quickly in my life. Rachel and Cora were right behind me, swimming just as quickly.

We swam through the gates of Neptunia, and immediately the festive sounds of Neptunia Day filled my ears.

The parade was over and night had fallen, but the celebrations would last until the last merpeople went home to their caves. There was music coming from games and rides all over the castle, everything from sea horse racing to seaweed necklace making to coral reef big wheels. It was absolutely magical. I wish I could stop and enjoy it, but there wasn't time.

I swam straight to the castle, but the guard at the front raised his hand as I approached. "The King and Queen have asked you to stay away while they deal with your mother's transgression," he said in a deep, solemn voice.

"Come with us," Cora's mum said. I turned to see that Cora's whole family and Rachel and her dad were behind us. Cora's mum was still clinging tightly to Jewel.

"We will all be at the Bell residence," she said to the guard. "Please ask the King and Queen to inform Shyanna's mother that we will wait there for her. She's a hero."

We swam through the castle, swimming past merpeople old and young who were smiling and enjoying Neptunia Day festivities. No one seemed to notice the look on my face. They all smiled and waved.

Thankfully they had no idea what had happened. They had no idea that the entire Mermaid Kingdom was nearly exposed to the human world. If anyone found out, it would be complete chaos.

We swam inside Cora's family cave, and her mum disappeared to put the babies to bed while her dad made us some hot chocolate.

After I had the last sip of my hot chocolate, my mum came swimming into the living room. I swam up to meet her. She held out her arms, and I slipped inside.

"Oh, Mum," I said, sobbing. She'd saved me and Jewel from being exposed, and for that I was grateful. But I felt guilty. If only I could have saved Jewel more quickly none of this would have happened.

Mum patted my tangled hair, her arms wrapped tightly around me. "It's okay, sweetheart," she whispered. "It's okay." I felt a little bit like a merbaby instead of a teenage mermaid.

"But you'll never walk on land again," I said. Tears ran down my cheeks like a waterfall.

"Oh, Shyanna," Mum said. "I haven't been on land for a long time anyway."

"But you could've gone if you'd wanted to up until now," I said. "And that's a big difference."

"It doesn't matter, Shy," she said. "It really doesn't

59

matter much to me. I was so worried about you and baby Jewel being caught, and I couldn't lose you. I won't. Not you, too." She squeezed me tighter, and I knew we were both thinking about my dad.

I pulled back from her and looked into her eyes. "Your voice," I said. "Even from below, it was the most amazing sound. Rachel's dad said it was the most wonderful voice he's ever heard. And that's from a singing teacher."

"That's an exaggeration," she said, blushing and looking shyly at the group.

"I don't think so," I said. "Those humans were mesmerized. They didn't know what was happening. That's why they dropped the net." I hugged her tightly again and then pulled out of her arms. "Thank you, Mum. Thank you for saving us."

Cora's mum was crying. She swam over and embraced both of us. "It's my fault. I should have gone," Cora's mum said. "You saved my baby's life. And I did nothing."

My mum shook her head. "No. You were protecting the rest of your family. I was the closest to the surface. And my husband always used to tell me my voice could save us from humans if we were ever spotted. I've always been too shy, but he used to love going off on treasure hunts and singing. Oh, how he'd sing. He would sing day and night."

She stared off into space for a moment, remembering him. "It had to be me," she whispered.

Cora's dad swam over and circled all of us in his arms. We were all shedding salty tears, both happy and sad at the same time.

"Crazy catfish!" Cora shouted, startling all of us out of our group hug.

We all stared at Cora. "Do you realize what time it is?" she cried again, pointing at the shell clock on the wall. "There's less than an hour until midnight!" she screamed. "And it's Shyanna's thirteenth birthday. We have to get her to the beach!"

Everyone started talking at once.

"Oh my goodness, I haven't even made her shrimp cake!" my mum cried.

"And her presents are still at home," Rachel called back.

"Never mind all that! It can wait. Her leg ceremony can't!" Cora pointed out. Thank goodness for Cora. She was always the sensible one.

My mum started to cry again. "I didn't even help you choose your song or outfit, and I missed our spa date." She hid her face in her hands. "I'm so sorry, Shyanna. I was so busy with the parade problems, and then all of this. And now I can't even take you onto land."

"You saved my life, Mum," I said. "I'll forgive you."

"She's right. You saved my sister and your daughter, so we'll feel sorry about Shyanna's birthday party later," Cora said. "At this moment, we need to focus on getting her to land."

"Perhaps we should clean her up at a bit first," Rachel said nicely.

They all looked at me, and I looked down at myself. I was a mess. My manicure was in shreds, my hair was all over the place and my once-shimmering tail was tattered and torn.

"No," I said quietly. "There isn't time."

"You're right," Rachel said. "It doesn't matter what you look like. I mean, you're beautiful, just a little ... um ... messy. All that matters is that you're there. On land. At midnight."

"No," I repeated, a little louder.

My mum put an arm around me. "The girls can go onto land with you. I know it was supposed to be me. But it's okay. They are your best friends."

I shook my head again. "NO!" I said, even louder this time. Everyone stopped to stare at me.

"It's okay," I said. "I don't need to get my legs." Rachel and Cora's mouths dropped open. "If my mum isn't able to leave the sea, I don't want to either."

"But Shyanna," Rachel said. "You've been so

excited about going onto land. It's all you've been talking about for weeks."

"Years, actually," Cora said.

I crossed my arms and shook my head. "No. I don't want to go onto land without my mum."

Rachel started to cry. "But Shyanna! You and Cora are my best friends, and land and legs are half of who I am. Cora and I have been waiting for your thirteenth birthday so that we can visit Owen on land together."

My mum swam forwards and put both hands on my cheeks. She leaned her forehead up against mine. "No, Shy," she said. "Your dad would want you to go onto land. He loved having legs. He loved taking me to the beach. I hoped I'd go with you, but I can't. I won't let you miss out on this part of your life for me."

"But mum... " I started to say.

"No. I insist, Shyanna. Please. Do it for me. Do it for your dad." She let me go and swam over and put one arm around Rachel and the other arm around Cora. "Do it for your best friends. But mostly, do it for you. It's what you've always wanted, and you deserve it."

Everyone was staring at me. Watching me. Waiting.

"Okay," I finally said. "But there's something I have to do first, before we go onto land. There's someone I need to talk to."

"Well, you'd better be quick," Cora said.

"Follow me," was my reply as I quickly swam out of the door.

Chapter nine

I swam towards the royal courtyard. Rachel, Cora, my mum and Rachel's dad followed me without speaking. Cora's parents stayed at home with the girls.

Even though it was almost midnight, Neptunia festivities were still going strong. We quickly swam to the entrance.

"Will you wait here?" I asked my mum. She frowned but nodded, and Rachel's dad said he would wait with her.

Rachel, Cora and I swam to the royal guard. I whispered to him what I wanted to do.

He nodded and swam ahead, leading us into the courtyard. Rachel and Cora each took one of my hands, and we swam together to the Queen. When she spotted us, she left her royal guests and swam over to greet us. She smiled when she reached us.

"Your baby sister is okay?" she asked Cora.

Cora nodded and squeezed my hand.

"What you did today was brave," the Queen said to me. "Swimming into the net to get Jewel out." She nodded at all three of us. "You mergirls are a constant surprise to the kingdom. Great singers, great spirit and true bravery."

"Thank you," we all said. I bowed my head. Rachel and Cora did the same thing.

"May I ask a favour," I asked the Queen as humbly as I could.

The Queen nodded. "Is it about your mother?" she guessed.

I nodded. "Yes."

I took a deep breath before I continued. "I know she wasn't supposed to expose herself to humans, but we all know she only did it to save me. She saved me and baby Jewel from being exposed and captured. If she hadn't done that, I wouldn't be here – neither would baby Jewel.

The Queen nodded again. "I know, Shyanna. You are very lucky."

"Her voice saved us," I said. "It was beautiful. It's such a shame she hasn't sung in such a long time. It wasn't easy for her to do it. She hasn't sung since my dad…"

I lowered my eyes to the sand at the bottom of the sea. The Queen glanced at the King, who was sitting in his throne juggling sea sponges while a group of admirers cheered.

"I would like to hear her sing one day. Perhaps I could even sing with her." She turned back to me. "Aren't you supposed to be somewhere?" She glanced at my messed-up tail and my crazy hairdo. I saw her hide a smile. "Tonight is your leg ceremony, isn't it?"

"It's supposed to be," I said.

She frowned ever so slightly.

"I was supposed to go onto land with my mum," I said. "I would still love to do that. She's all I have. I don't have a dad anymore, and I don't have any siblings. I only have my mum."

The Queen sighed.

"Is there any way you can use magic?" I asked. "Can you reverse her spell so she can use her legs again? She saved two lives! It was a selfless act. There must be exceptions. Can you please help me? Please?" I begged.

The Queen clicked her tongue, glanced at the King again, and then back to me.

"I wish I could help you," she said finally, "but I can't reverse the spell that quickly. No one can. It has to be done in stages. Other royalty will need to help – if they agree at all. It would have to go to a vote,

which takes time," she added and then looked into my eyes. "You must go, Shyanna. Time is ticking. It's midnight tonight or it will be too late to get your legs. That spell can never be reversed."

Rachel and Cora each grabbed one of my hands again. I needed the support.

"But my mum," I said.

"Go on," the Queen said. "Go and get your legs. I will discuss this matter with the King. I can't promise you anything. But we will discuss it, you have my word."

"Thank you," I said with a bow.

The girls pulled me away, but I glanced over my shoulder at the Queen as we left the courtyard. She was already at the King's side. He caught my eye and winked. I'd done what I could. Now it was time to go.

"Come on!" Cora said. "It's getting late. We are running out of time!"

Outside the castle, the girls let go of my hands,

and my mum took one. "Is everything okay?" she asked me.

"I hope so," I whispered.

On the way to the beach, Mum asked me what I'd planned for the leg ceremony. I told her all about my spa day and the plans I had made with Star. When I had finished, she started to sing. Goosebumps ran along my arms, down my back, and all the way down my tail. Her voice was simply incredible. Rachel's dad swam to my other side, and he joined in and sang with her. It was perfect.

As the song ended, we were approaching the beach. Mum let go of my hand. "Go," she said. "I can't go any further. Your friends will go with you."

Rachel's dad stayed with her, but Cora and Rachel swam up with me. The moonlight lit up the beach. It was breathtaking. There was a path of white flowers sparkling along the shore. I glanced at the girls.

"We all came up to decorate earlier as a surprise," Rachel said. "Just before Jewel got trapped."

"So that's why you were all out? That's when Jewel got trapped in the net. It was all for me?" I asked.

"Did you think we'd forget your birthday?" Cora asked. "Don't be silly!"

"Come on, Shy. It's time," Rachel said, smiling.

I breathed in the night air, nervous and excited about what was about to happen. And then I opened my mouth and began to sing.

I saw Rachel and Cora grin. It was our song. The song we first sang together at the Melody Carnival. The song that would always represent our friendship.

Rachel and Cora swam slowly next to me, and then they stepped out of the water. I blinked, and they had their legs. Lovely long, graceful limbs.

They walked up to the beach on the flower path and turned, waiting for me. I moved slowly forwards. My tail began to tingle. It got heavier and heavier, and then a strange sensation ran down my middle. It didn't hurt. It just felt odd.

A breeze hit my legs, and I looked down and realized my tail had disappeared. I was wearing a swimming costume, the same colour and texture as my tail. But instead of a fin, I had feet. I had toes. I even had knees. I lifted one leg, shook it out a little, and began to laugh.

"Walk!" Rachel shouted, and they both clapped and called out encouragement. I tried to take another step and fell flat on my face.

"That's exactly what I did!" Cora squealed. "Try again."

I laughed and got up on my knees.

"Try again!" Cora screeched. "It gets easier!"

Rachel ran further up the beach. "Come on, Shyanna!"

I got up off of my knees, wobbling a little and then finding balance on my feet.

"Wow!" I said. And then I took a step and then another. "I'm doing it!" I cried. "I'm walking."

"Oh, yes you are!" Cora ran to my side.

"Have fun, girls!" a voice called out from under the sea.

My mum. I couldn't see her, but I knew she was there. Watching and smiling.

"Be back before morning," she called.

"We will," I shouted into the night air. The oxygen filled my lungs in a different way than the sea water did. It made me light-headed, and I giggled and threw out my arms and kicked my new legs.

"It's too late for Owen to be here," Rachel said. "But we'll come back soon. The three of us."

The three of us skipped together in the dark night air, enjoying every minute. Before I knew it, the sun was rising. I glanced down at my legs, wiggled my toes, and then stepped back into the sea. There would be more adventures to be had on land soon.

I only hoped my mum would be able to be a part of them.

Chapter ten

"Wake-up, sleepyhead!" a voice called from outside my room.

I opened my eyes, and memories of the day before rushed into my head. It hadn't been exactly the birthday I'd planned, but it was still the best birthday I could imagine. There was drama, excitement, adventure and a happy ending.

I stretched my arms out over my head and remembered the feeling of having legs. I wiggled my tail around, happy to have it back but eager to try out my new legs again. The feeling was completely indescribable.

"We were all up late, but you must have worn yourself out having such a great time on land!" Mum said. "It's time to get up!"

"It was so much fun, though, especially skipping," I said, but then my heart sank a little, knowing she might never be able to go onto land again.

"Legs are so different from a tail," she said, swimming into my room and doing a somersault. "Breathing air always made me so giggly."

I nodded, watching her. She didn't look sad, but my heart still ached a little for her.

"Come on, Shyanna," she said. "I'll make fish-shaped pancakes for breakfast!"

"Okay!" I swam out of bed and flipped around the room to find a comfortable shell top to put on. Then I followed her into the kitchen.

"SURPRISE!" voices shouted when I swam into the kitchen.

I screamed in shock, and everyone started to laugh. Our kitchen was full of merboys and mergirls and their parents.

"Happy belated birthday!" everyone shouted. I glanced around, my hand still on my heart.

"Today you can have the party you were supposed to have yesterday!" my mum said as she swam to me and gave me a giant hug.

Rachel and Cora swam up too. "With pancakes and presents!" Cora shouted.

"And shrimp cake," Rachel added.

Everyone was chattering and smiling. It was amazing. I blushed at a loud rendition of "Happy Birthday," and my heart came close to bursting with happiness. Then someone pushed me into a decorated shell chair, and someone else started handing me presents to open.

"Oh my goodness," I said. "Birthday presents!"

"We know how much you love presents!" Cora said and laughed.

"And we heard that you saved Cora's baby sister," Cassie said. "That's amazing, Shyanna. You deserve lots of presents."

I glanced over at my mum. She put her finger on her lips to signal for me not to say anything about her role in the rescue of Jewel. Across the noisy room, our eyes locked for a moment and I smiled at her, so thankful to have her as my mum.

"How were your legs?" asked a classmate who hadn't yet turned thirteen as she handed me another present to open.

"Magical." I smiled. "Simply magical."

Everyone kept talking and laughing as I opened present after present, feeling like the luckiest mermaid in Mermaid Kingdom. As I was stuffing my face with another piece of shrimp cake, a hush went over the room. It went from noisy to quiet in a second. I turned from the table to see the Queen of Neptunia looking at me. She carried a scroll of paper in her hand.

I glanced behind her, but she was alone. No King or guard.

"Hello, Shyanna. I'm looking for your mother," she said formally. No one else in the room made a sound. Everyone's eyes were on the Queen. It was very surreal.

"Yes?" my mum said, looking confused. The crowd around me parted, and Mum floated up next to me and tucked my hand in hers, as if offering me moral support. I glanced at her face, but she looked calm, not as terrified and nervous as I felt.

"I come with news," the Queen announced. She turned to me. "Shyanna Angler has come to me and requested special use of Mermaid Magic to reverse the spell that has taken away your ability to use your legs on land."

Merpeople around the room gasped, and a low whisper buzzed as they gossiped about what had happened. The Queen lifted her hand, and the room fell silent again.

"Last night, the King and I called an emergency session with the Royal Council to discuss this interesting situation."

I held my breath.

She stared at my mum. "We've reached a decision."

No one said a word. I didn't even hear anyone take a breath. The Queen waited an extra moment for dramatic effect. She loved to perform, the Queen. She cleared her throat and opened the scroll and began reading from it.

"The Royal Council has decided to grant Emerald Angler use of her legs, even though she was seen by humans."

Everyone in the room gasped and started whispering.

The Queen held up her hand and waited for quiet.

"It is due to special circumstances. Two mermaid lives were saved, and thus we have decided to alter the magic for leg use. But there will be strict stipulations."

I squeezed my mum's hand tightly. My heart

pounded so loudly I was sure everyone in the room could hear it.

"Emerald will be allowed to use legs on land, but only when accompanied by either mermaid she saved, Shyanna Angler or Jewel Bass."

The room erupted in chatter again.

"Did she save Jewel?" some people asked. "What happened? Which humans saw her?"

The Queen finished, and she rolled up the scroll and swam forwards, ignoring the chaos in the room. She swam up to my mum and me, smiled, and handed the scroll to my mum.

"What you did was very brave. I see where your daughter gets her bravery from," the Queen said to my mum. She winked at me.

"I would like to hear you sing soon," she said to my mum. "Perhaps a duet?"

My mum nodded quickly, and the Queen smiled and bowed her head.

"Thank you so much," I said. I grinned. "Can I

offer you and the King a slice of birthday cake? You can take it back to him."

"Salmon cake?" she asked.

"Shrimp," I told her.

"The King and I do love a good shrimp cake," she said and patted my head.

I cut two large slices and wrapped them up. By the time I had finished, the Queen was laughing with my mum about something. I handed her the cake. "Thank you again," I said.

She accepted the cake. "The King is sorry he couldn't come along. He had a round of sea golf booked with another king and couldn't get out of it." She smiled brightly. "Try and stay out of trouble now," she said.

And then she was gone.

Mum put her mouth close to my ear. "After the party is over, you and I are going onto land," she whispered.

"Are you sure?" I asked. It would be her first time on land since my dad had disappeared.

"It's time," she said.

Rachel and Cora swam over, and we squealed with delight. I looked at my mum. "Is it okay if my best friends come?"

She nodded. "I wouldn't want it any other way. These girls are like family!"

I told Rachel and Cora what we were going to do, and then we twirled in circles and did flips of excitement.

It was the best belated birthday party anyone had ever had. Even my biggest, best dreams couldn't compare. All of my wishes had come true.

Legend of mermaids

These creatures of the sea have many secrets. Although people have believed in mermaids for centuries, nobody has ever proven their existence. People all over the world are attracted to mysterious mermaids.

The earliest mermaid story dates back to around 1000 BC in an Assyrian legend. A goddess loved a human man but killed him accidentally. She fled to the water in shame. She tried to change into a fish, but the water would not let her hide her true nature. She lived the rest of her days as half-woman, half-fish.

Later, the ancient Greeks whispered tales of fishy women called sirens. These beautiful but deadly beings lured sailors to their graves. Many sailors feared or respected mermaids because of their association with doom.

Note: This text was taken from *The Girl's Guide to Mermaids: Everything Alluring about These Mythical Beauties* by Sheri A. Johnson (Capstone Press, 2012).

Talk about it

1. Shyanna couldn't wait to be thirteen and get her legs. What birthday are you looking forward to the most? Why?

2. There was lots of drama on Shyanna's birthday — from being alone, to saving Jewel, to her mum losing her land privileges — it was a very busy day! Discuss how you think Shyanna coped with everything?

3. Do you think it was a good idea for Shyanna's mum to break the rules and distract the humans? What else could have been done?

4. Were you surprised that the Queen reversed the ruling about Shyanna's mum and her ability to go onto land again? Why or why not?

Write it down

1. If you could do anything in the world for your birthday, what would it be? Write a detailed description of your dream birthday.

2. Being a mermaid sounds like fun, but it also seems dangerous. Using examples from the book, write a "for" and "against" list about being a mermaid. Discuss your list with your friends.

3. Write a newspaper article about the big rescue of baby Jewel.

4. Pretend you are Shyanna and write a diary entry about your birthday. Ensure you include details about how you were feeling during each event of the day.

About the author

Janet Gurtler has written many well-received books for the Young Adult market. Mermaid Kingdom is her first series for younger readers. She lives near the Canadian Rockies in Calgary, Canada, with her husband, son and a chubby Chihuahua called Bruce.

About the illustrator

Katie Wood fell in love with drawing
when she was very young. Since graduating
from Loughborough University School
of Art and Design in 2004, she has been
living her dream working as a freelance
illustrator. From her studio in Leicester,
she creates bright and lively illustrations for
books and magazines all over the world.

Dive in and get swept away!